THE WATER GIFT
AND THE PIG OF THE PIG

Jacqueline Briggs Martin

Illustrated by Linda S. Wingerter

HOUGHTON MIFFLIN COMPANY

BOSTON 2003

To all those who listen for the earth talking
—J.B.M.

For GG, Pepi, Apple, and Bill
—L.S.W.

www.houghtonmifflinbooks.com

The text of this book is set in Filosophia.
The illustrations are acrylic.

Library of Congress Cataloging-in-Publication Data

Martin, Jacqueline Briggs.
The water gift and the pig of the pig / by Jacqueline Briggs Martin;
illustrated by Linda S. Wingerter.
p. cm.
Summary: An orphan girl discovers that she shares her grandfather's gift for finding things
when their very clever pig disappears.
ISBN 0-618-07436-8
[1. Pigs—Fiction. 2. Dowsing—Fiction. 3. Grandfathers—Fiction. 4. Orphans—Fiction.]
I. Wingerter, Linda S., ill. II. Title.
PZ7.M363168 Wat 2003
[E]—dc21 00-059742

Manufactured in the United States of America
WOZ 10 9 8 7 6 5 4 3 2 1

ABOUT THE WATER GIFT

For many centuries there have been those, including children, who could locate underground water (and sometimes gold or silver, lost people or animals) by walking across the ground holding a Y-shaped branch. The long end of the branch points down when it is over underground water. Sometimes the forked branch is called a "divining rod," sometimes a "dowsing stick." No one knows how this works, or why it works for some and not others. For those who love the mysteries of this world, the water gift is a source of wonder and delight.

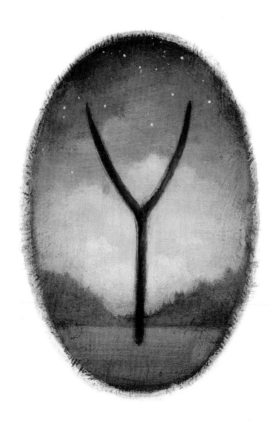

MY GRANDFATHER IS A WATER MAN.

He went to sea on a sailing ship

when he was ten years old.

He was captain of the big schooner *Arundel* when he was twenty-five.

But he left the ship and left the sea to marry my grandmother.

He kept a captain's coat that he still wears on rainy days.

He kept schooner stories he tells after supper,

and he kept the Pig That Went Around Cape Horn.

"Isabel," he'll say to me, "that Pig followed me like a dog.

She was smart enough to smell a storm coming.

And she danced with the first mate when the storm was over."

Grandmother says the Pig thought she was family

and slept on the rug by the cook stove.

She's gone now, but we have the last pig of her last litter—

the Pig of the Pig That Went Around Cape Horn.

She is smart enough to count to five.

She follows me like a dog

and sits in the front of the boat

when Grandfather and I go fishing for haddock.

I would say the Pig of the Pig is my best friend.

We have a secret handshake.

The Pig of the Pig doesn't care

that I never win races or spelling contests.

She doesn't care that I won't climb trees with my cousins,

and don't talk as much as a mouse in a corner.

The Pig and I like to go to the hundred-year tree in the lane.

We watch birds and chase butterflies. She hums while I sing.

I stand on the rock I call *Arundel*. We sail it out to sea.

"Do you smell a Cape Horn storm coming?" I say in Grandfather's voice.

"With wind that cuts like scissors and saw blades?
Fix your eye on a powerful star and Cook's hot soup.
We'll get through."

And we always go with Grandfather when he works the water gift.

Perhaps because he loves water so much,

Grandfather can find it

even when it's hidden under fields and pastures.

He takes a Y-shaped branch,

holds the forked ends in his hands,

and walks back and forth across a field.

When the long end turns down,

Grandfather says, "Dig here," and there is water.

Grandfather doesn't know how he finds the water

or how his friend Ezra Littlefield once found a stray cow.

He just knows the stick turns down

and can't be stopped. It's a mystery.

Grandfather says it's the whole earth talking.

This summer Lovejoy the apple man asked for Grandfather's help.

Lovejoy has plenty of trees,

but his apples were stunted and wormy

because they didn't get enough water in dry weather.

Grandfather walked the orchard until the stick pointed down.

Our neighbor Ben Stinchfield, mean as his little biter dog, said,

"There won't be water."

Grandfather says Ben Stinchfield doesn't believe in gifts.

He wouldn't give away the good smell

from a piece of warm toast.

Lovejoy didn't listen to Ben Stinchfield,

and when he dug, he found water—

right where Grandfather said he would.

Lovejoy called Grandfather "The Water King of Waldo County"

and promised to bring us a bushel of his best apples.

Then bad luck rained down like a three-day storm.
Grandfather found a well for neighbors
and Ben Stinchfield laughed when the water tasted like swamp tea.
Grandfather spent two days on Snell's Hill and didn't find a drop.
Worst, he fell off the top of a hay wagon, and he hurt to walk.
People stopped coming by to ask for the water gift.
Grandfather just sat. He wouldn't tell schooner stories.
When Lovejoy brought the bushel of apples in the fall,
I heard Grandfather say he had lost the gift.
He tossed his Y-shaped branch into the fire.

After that, nothing was the same.
The Pig of the Pig and I went to our tree,
but the rock I called *Arundel* was just a rock.
One morning I found the Pig
sitting in the boat, waiting to fish for haddock.
"Not today," Grandfather said. "My bones are too tired."
The Pig of the Pig stopped humming.

Then came the day she didn't show up for noon dinner.

"Let's go find our Pig," I said.

"She knows the way back," Grandfather said. "She'll come home."

I went to the stone wall and saw a gap in the rocks.

Perhaps she had followed a bird into Stinchfield's woods.

My cousins would have searched from the top of a tree.

I waited under the hundred-year tree until dark.

The next day Ben Stinchfield banged on the door.

"Someone saw your pig in my woods," he said.

"If I catch her she'll be mine." And he stomped out.

I knew Ben Stinchfield was thinking of bacon

and ham, pork chops, and pigskin gloves.

Grandmother put on her determination hat

and we went out together.

We looked in the pasture. We walked the woods.

We called until we could only whisper.

But we did not find our Pig.

The next day came up windy enough to rattle doorknobs.

Grandfather sat by the fireplace.

He didn't build a fire until I brought in the wood.

Grandmother kept busy making apple pies.

"Put out some turnips," Grandfather said.

"Our Pig will come for turnips."

By noon, no Pig had come and the sky looked mean and lowery.

I heard Stinchfield walking the woods and calling, "Here, Pig. Here, Pig."

Don't answer. Don't answer, I whispered.

The cold wind blew like a Cape Horn storm,

but I could not go inside.

We had tried food.

We had tried walking and calling—and waiting.

There was only one thing left to do.

First, I would have to climb the hundred-year tree.

I jumped and fell. Jumped again—and grabbed.

My knees were bumped; my hands were scraped

by the time I got myself out of that tree

and ran to Grandfather.

"Ezra Littlefield found a cow. We'll find our Pig," I told him.

"You never quit in those Cape Horn storms.

We can't quit on the Pig of the Pig."

Grandfather looked at the forked branch in my hand.

He stood up and buttoned the top button of my coat

as if I might be cold.

"We'll try, Isabel."

We headed toward the woods

and crossed through the gap in the stone wall.

He put my hand on one side of the branch

and we walked, step by slow step.

Grandfather said, "Is the Pig of the Pig to the north?"

The stick stayed pointing up.

"Is the Pig to the east?" I said.

Perhaps it was just my shivering hand.

Perhaps it was the wind.

But the stick wavered.

We held tight.

The stick pointed down and we turned east.

We walked over rough ground, past brush and boulders.

And there was our Pig—at the far side of the woods, fallen into a hole.

It's a wonder that Stinchfield hadn't found her.

He and his biter dog would have walked past that hole

every time he went into the woods.

But Ben Stinchfield does not believe in the earth talking.

When we pulled her up,

the Pig of the Pig was limpy and worn out.

Both ears were bent down, and she was splotched with mud.

She remembered the secret handshake, though,

and she did a little three-legged skip. You might call it a dance.

I danced too.

Then we went home to Grandmother's kitchen
for hot soup and apple pie.

My Grandfather has the water gift. And so do I.
Annie Bates has asked us to find a well for her chicken farm.
And she promised to pay with oak wood.
Grandfather says we'll build a sailing ship
in the barn this winter.

Next summer he will teach me to sail.
And the Pig of the Pig will hum
and—once in a while—
dance her three-legged dance on the deck.